J FICTION W (NEW) (AIT)

JAMES THE ROCK'S BOYS

BY **THALIA WIGGINS**
ILLUSTRATED BY **DON TATE**

Published by Magic Wagon, a division of the ABDO Group, PO Box 398166, Minneapolis, Minnesota 55439. Copyright © 2012 by Abdo Consulting Group, Inc. International copyrights reserved in all countries. All rights reserved. No part of this book may be reproduced in any form without written permission from the publisher.

Calico Chapter Books™ is a trademark and logo of Magic Wagon.

Printed in the United States of America, North Mankato, Minnesota.
102011
012012

 This book contains at least 10% recycled materials.

Text by Thalia Wiggins
Illustrations by Don Tate
Edited by Stephanie Hedlund and Rochelle Baltzer
Cover and interior design by Neil Klinepier

Library of Congress Cataloging-in-Publication Data

Wiggins, Thalia, 1983-
  James the Rock's boys / by Thalia Wiggins ; illustrated by Don Tate.
     p. cm. -- (Making choices : the McNair cousins)
  Summary: Even though he is jealous of his cousin Greg's success in the mural competition, James and his gang of friends set out to trap the vandals who have defaced the artwork.
  ISBN 978-1-61641-635-5
  1. Cousins--Juvenile fiction. 2. Jealousy--Juvenile fiction. 3. Decision making in adolescence--Juvenile fiction. 4. Vandalism--Juvenile fiction. 5. Trinidad--Juvenile fiction. [1. Cousins--Fiction. Jealousy--Fiction. 3. Decision making--Fiction. 4. Vandalism--Fictio 5. Trinidad--Fiction.] I. Tate, Don, ill. II. Title.
  PZ7.W63856Jd 2012
  813.6--dc23
                                        2011027717

Cont███

A Star Is Born

"What's up, man?" Moochie bumped James's fist as they met in front of the doors at school. "Did I just see you jump out of your grandpa's van?"

"Yeah." James pretended to catch his breath. "April was driving. My life was flashing before my eyes!"

"So did Greg win the mural contest yet?" Moochie asked.

"Nah. He was supposed to get a letter in the mail over a week ago." James rolled his eyes. "I've been hearing about the letter all week! I just want to see if he won already!"

James stopped at his locker. "So, Coach Jennings called my house. He told Grandpa I may have a shot on the basketball team this year. Grandpa said I could try out as long as I keep my grades up and stay out of trouble."

"Good luck!" Moochie joked. James reached out to hit him and missed.

"Coach Jennings called my house last night, too." Troy walked up and pulled books out of his locker. "Are you going to practice after school?" he asked James.

"Of course!" James looked at his friends. "It beats getting into trouble," he said half-seriously.

When the bell rang at the end of the school day, they made their way to the basketball court at the recreation center. In minutes, they were teamed up and tossing a basketball around.

"Come on, Moochie!" James called as Moochie missed another layup. "You can do it!"

Moochie cursed and chased the ball. "I'm just no good!" he said to James through clenched teeth. "You and Troy are the stars! I'll never be as good as you two!"

"That may be true!" James joked. "But you have great speed! You just need to believe in yourself!"

They practiced an hour longer. Moochie started to relax and improved his game. James and the others cheered him on.

"We knew you could do it!" Randy playfully punched Moochie in the arm.

"All you needed was confidence," James added.

"Thanks for believing in me, James!" Moochie gave him a high-five.

"Anytime!" James felt good for helping his friend. "Just don't think you'll ever be as good as me!" he joked.

Winner!

"Please don't kill me!" James pretended to cry while April pulled off from the curb. Charles laughed.

"You can always walk, you know!" April readjusted the rearview mirror.

"Easy, easy." Grandpa coached April as she pulled into traffic.

James turned to Charles. "How about a couple hours of Basketball Jam after dinner? I owe you a whipping!"

"How about a couple hours of homework before video games!" Grandpa said.

James rolled his eyes. Charles winked at him.

Without warning, the van hit a pothole. James cursed.

"James!" Grandpa barked. "Be careful, April."

April successfully pulled into the driveway. She beamed at Grandpa. She looked at James and stuck out her tongue.

As they approached the door, Greg opened it.

"Hey, Greg," Charles puffed, as he practiced using his crutches. "Did your letter come today?"

"Yeah!" Greg held it up for everyone to see. "I won!"

James felt a pang of jealousy, but he joined in when the family cheered for Greg.

Grandma looked at her watch. James noticed she looked like she wanted to stay and celebrate. "I've got to go to work. Why don't you all have pizza tonight? Love you all!"

"Congrats, Greg!" Grandpa patted Greg on the back.

"Yeah, man!" James slapped Greg's back a little too hard.

"Alright! You guys stop it." Grandpa laughed. "Someone order the pizza."

Daydreams

Soon it was Saturday morning—the day of the opening festivities for Greg's mural.

"James, wake up!" Grandpa banged on James's bedroom door and opened it. Then, he moved on to Greg's room.

"Ugh," James groaned. He rolled over and looked at his clock.

"Man, it's early!" James exclaimed. He pulled the covers back over his head. "Grandpa, can I sleep in and meet y'all later? It's only a few blocks away."

"No, you cannot sleep in!" Grandpa came in James's room. "Get up now! This is for Greg! He's worked so hard."

James sucked his teeth and got up while Grandpa watched. He finally left when James went to his closet.

"Greg this and Greg that!" James hissed. "There's more than one grandchild living here!" he muttered.

An hour later they were all at the community center. James immediately found Moochie.

"Wow! There sure are a lot of people here," Moochie remarked when James joined him. He motioned to the crowds of journalists, police, volunteers, and neighbors.

James was impressed. He realized how many people were here for his cousin. He felt jealous again. *Greg is getting all this attention! I wish the camera crews and journalists were here for me!* he thought.

He shrugged off his feelings and headed to the front of the aisles.

"What contest is this again?" Troy yawned.

James found himself yawning, too. "After they finished remodeling the community center, Ms. Robinson, the art teacher, suggested that Greg enter the contest to have a mural painted on this large wall out here in the garden area." James motioned to a wall that was covered by a huge cloth.

"Wasn't the name of the contest called 'My Dreams of Tomorrow Today'?" Moochie asked.

"Yeah," James answered. "Greg decided to draw us as adults in our careers. Y'all know I want to be a ball player, so Greg drew me doing a slam dunk. He also drew his best friend, Alex, as a businessman in a suit. And he drew himself as a graphic designer."

"Cool." His friends looked mesmerized.

"Anyway," James playfully pushed Troy forward. "Walk faster." They made their way to where the McNairs were gathered. James noticed that Greg was talking to a girl and blushing.

James chuckled at his cousin and pointed. "There's Greg's friend, Alex, and that fine girl must be Alex's little sister, Marina." He shook his head and listened to Greg.

When Greg was finished, James silently moved forward in his chair and said near Greg's ear, "Man, you really need to learn how to talk to girls!"

Greg jumped. James and his friends laughed until there were tears in their eyes.

James tuned out most of what the mayor said. He knew it would be about how good Greg was. He rolled his eyes as the mayor invited Greg to the stage and there was a round of applause.

Grandpa turned in his chair and gave James and his friends a look that meant to stand up and cheer or else. James was the last one to stand up. He looked up at Greg, who stood beaming at the crowd. He felt both jealousy and something else . . . like hope.

Maybe if I get my act together and focus on basketball, I could have all this attention,

James thought. *I could actually BE a star!* He imagined himself as a basketball player. He would be in the NBA and unstoppable on the court. He would be voted MVP and, of course, be rich!

James broke out of his daydream in time to see Greg and the mayor cut the ribbon to blinding flashes of cameras.

I can't wait until those cameras flash for me! James thought.

The Crush 'Em Boys

The next day, James and his friends made their way to the recreation center after school. They practiced for an hour.

"Great job, guys!" James heard a familiar voice that made his heart skip a beat. It was Coach Jennings. He had been watching James and his friends practice.

"McNair!" Coach Jennings called. James trotted over.

"Yes, Coach?" James tried not to look nervous.

"You did excellent out there! I'm impressed." He smiled at James. "Try-outs are in a couple of weeks, but I can tell now that you would make an excellent point guard."

James's jaw dropped. He quickly recovered and beamed. "Yes, sir!"

"Troy!" Coach Jennings called. Troy came over, biting his lip.

"Y-yes?" Troy stuttered.

"You did well with McNair out there." He nodded to James. "I would love for you to try out. I hope you two are as good at being teammates as you are as friends."

Troy cheered and high-fived James. April, Greg, and Charles joined them minutes later. They all made their way home.

James was too excited to speak as they left. He kept thinking about being a basketball star. He would make a lot of money.

Maybe Grandpa will finally be proud of me, James thought.

As they passed the convenience store, they noticed fresh graffiti on the wall.

"Crush 'Em Boys?" James sucked his teeth. "Who are those clowns?"

"Some wannabe tough boys our age who live on the top of the hill," Moochie said.

"They're crazy if they think they can just come in our neighborhood and start tagging walls!" Troy declared.

"Yeah, they know better than to mess with us!" James held up his arms and flexed his muscles.

"Rock's Boys will crush and mush them Crush 'Em Boys!" Moochie said.

"So what are you going to do?" Greg asked, half-jokingly. "Go in their neighborhood and tag their walls?"

"Hey, we do what we have to do to let them know we're not scared of them!"

"Yeah," Moochie said. "We do what we have to do!" He turned to James. "What are we going to do, though?"

Greg, April, and Charles looked at each other and rolled their eyes.

James dropped off his backpack at home and walked with Moochie to the corner store. Moochie's older brother, Ken, was standing outside, along with some other boys not much older than James.

Ken hugged Moochie and playfully hit him on the head. Then he turned to James. "Yo, Rock! You know some boys called the Crush 'Em Boys are spraying buildings in our neighborhood?"

"Yeah!" James said angrily. "They don't know who they're messing with!"

He put up his fists to show what he meant. Everyone nodded and laughed.

"So, what are you going to do?" Ken asked him.

"I don't know. I wish I could find the boys who've been tagging our walls!" James shrugged. "All I know is that they live on top of the hill."

"So what are you waiting for?" Ken pointed to the hill. "Go up there and start spraying their walls. See how they like it!" The other boys agreed.

James felt a pit in his stomach. He knew that people were expecting him to retaliate against the Crush 'Em Boys. But he couldn't forget the happiness he felt when Coach Jennings told him he may have a spot on the basketball team.

If I get into serious trouble with the police, I won't have a chance on the team, he thought. *On the other hand, Ken is the toughest boy in our hood. I don't want to look like I'm scared of the Crush 'Em Boys!*

"Here." Moochie's brother looked to see if anyone else was around. One of his friends pulled out a brown paper bag and handed it to James.

James took it nervously. He didn't know whether or not he wanted to see what was inside the bag. Whatever it was, he knew it would be bad. He reached in and pulled out a can of spray paint.

"What did you think it was?" Ken noticed the relieved look on his face.

"Nothing." James swallowed hard.

"Don't worry, Rock!" Ken saluted him. "You don't have to look for them. Once you start tagging their walls, they'll come to you!"

"Yeah." James's throat felt dry. *The problem is I don't want to tag their walls in the first place!* he thought. He pretended to be grateful and bumped fists with Moochie's brother.

The Rock Meets Mark

The next day, there was another event at the community center. James, Troy, and Moochie had to go home and get their bikes first. The air was starting to get cold.

"You know if you get caught, Rock, you won't be on the team," Troy said with concern in his voice.

"I know that!" James pedaled his bike slower so they could talk. "What do you want me to do? I can't just let them tag our neighborhood."

"Why don't we just leave the problem alone and do nothing?" Moochie said in between breaths. "Maybe the Crush 'Em Boys will find someone else to pick on and leave us alone."

James passed another Crush 'Em Boy tag on a stop sign. "I don't think so."

"But that means you'll have to fight or something to prove you're still big and bad!" Moochie squealed. "What if you get hurt?"

"What?" James almost laughed. "Me get hurt? I wish I could get my hands on a Crush 'Em Boy! I would break him into pieces!"

James didn't know his chance to meet a Crush 'Em Boy would come so soon. Later that afternoon when he and the boys were biking home from practice, James spotted a boy messing with Greg.

"What's going on?" James got off his bike and into the boy's face. The boy was as tall as he was, but James showed no fear. "Who are you?"

"I'm Mark—as in I always hit my mark!" he raised his fists up to show what he meant.

"Oh, really?" James burst into laughter.

"He doesn't know who he's messing with, right, Rock?" Troy said.

Mark smiled wickedly at James. "So you're Rock, eh? We at the top of the hill have been waiting to meet you!"

James was surprised. "You're a Crush 'Em Boy?"

"That's right!" Mark pushed James. "So you better watch out or—"

James had Mark on the ground before Greg could yell, "No!"

"Looks like the Crush 'Em Boy got crushed!" James laughed. His friends joined in the laughter.

Mark sprung up and grabbed his bike. "I'm going to get you, Rock!"

"It's a long way up the hill!" James teased.

Greg looked at the bike in the distance. "I think you just started something with the Crush 'Em Boys, don't you?"

James felt cold. Things were happening too fast. Now he had his first run-in with the Crush 'Em Boys and he knew things were going to get worse. He tried not to look scared.

"Whatever those chumps have, we'll be ready for them! Right guys?"

James walked over to his friends.

"Yeah! Rock's Boys!" His friends cheered again.

Greg did not look convinced. Neither was James.

A Not-So-Good Plan

That night, James was getting ready to join his family in the living room to watch Greg on TV again.

"Greg gets another interview. Big deal!" James muttered while gathering a pile of dirty clothes. He tripped over his backpack, causing clothes to spill from his hands. He kicked it, and out fell the brown paper bag containing the can of spray paint. The can slid out and rolled in front of his foot.

James gulped, feeling sick. He thought about Coach Jennings and his dream of playing basketball. But his hopes seemed dashed by the fight with Mark. He shoved the can back in his backpack and continued gathering laundry.

Once you start being a bad boy, it's hard to stop, James thought. *You do one wrong thing and bad consequences happen. It seems like I'll live a bad life forever! Besides, those Crush 'Em Boys are going to be looking for me. If I tell Grandpa or the police, then Mark will think I'm scared.*

James was still feeling frustrated when Moochie called. He picked up the phone and said, "Hey, Moochie, what's up?"

Moochie sighed and said, "I don't think you should tag the walls."

"Oh really?" James sat on his bed.

"Yeah, man. I love my brother, but he's been in trouble with the law so many times that I don't think you should take his advice."

"So what do you think I should do? Tell my Grandpa? Run to the police like a scaredy cat? Mark will think I'm scared of him and I'm not!" James hissed.

"But, Rock, someone could get hurt! Maybe we should tell the police."

"I'm not gonna have the whole neighborhood thinking I'm soft!" James bellowed into the receiver. "Your brother is right! I have to protect my image!"

James heard a noise. He looked over at his door and thought he saw someone standing outside it. He tiptoed to the door while continuing to talk.

"Moochie, don't be scared! When we're done with them, the Crush 'Em Boys won't know what hit them!"

James opened the door and Greg fell backward. James tried not to laugh.

"Moochie, let me call you back." He hung up.

"Well, well." James leaned down to his cousin. "Hear anything good?" He grabbed Greg's shirt by the collar and pulled him up.

"What are you going to do, James?" Greg struggled to get free. "Go out to their neighborhood and start trouble? That will just make things worse!"

"They need to know that they can't mess with us!" James let go of Greg.

"I'm not scared of Mark," Greg said. Then he thought about it. "Well, maybe I am a little."

"That's why we have to protect ourselves and to let them know that we won't back down!" James said.

Greg stared at James. Then he shook his head. Suddenly, he looked down and saw the can of spray paint poking out of James's backpack.

"Spray p—!" Greg started to say loudly, but James covered his mouth.

"Quiet!" James shushed.

"Can't breathe!" Greg struggled to speak. James released him.

"I can't believe you!" Greg's jaw dropped. "You're going to get yourself into more trouble."

"You wouldn't understand." James ushered Greg out into the hallway. He closed his bedroom door behind them.

"Not a word to Grandpa or I'll spray paint *Greg loves Marina* all over your mural!" James muttered as they went downstairs.

Greg stopped midway to face James. "You wouldn't!"

James chuckled and shoved him downstairs. "Now that you're a celebrity I guess the girls will come in by the thousands."

"It's on!" Charles announced as the boys entered the living room.

Everyone in the McNair household cheered for Greg. James offered a toast.

"To Greg," he announced, "the type of guy you can depend on!"

To be quiet! he wanted to add. He gave Greg a playful but serious look that no one else noticed.

Bad Cousin vs. Good Cousin

It didn't take long before James got into trouble. When he walked to the principal's office days later, he prayed it was because of the boy he and Troy had shoved in a locker at lunchtime.

James knew the principal's office well. He had been there many times. And each time seemed to feel a little worse, especially now, seeing Grandpa, Moochie, Troy, Randy, their families, the principal, and a police officer crowding the room.

James felt ashamed that he was the ringleader. He let everyone down.

The principal seated herself at her desk. She sighed and took off her glasses. "I'm disappointed in you four." She eyed each boy before turning to a computer monitor on her desk.

"Officer Jackson brought some video footage from a convenience store located up the hill." She signaled to the police officer standing by the door. He nodded.

She clicked a button. A video of James, Moochie, Troy, and Randy spray painting on a wall began on the screen.

Moochie groaned. James felt like someone had punched him in the stomach.

"I heard from some of my students that you four call yourselves Rock's Boys," The principal went on. She looked at them questioningly. They nodded.

"I also heard that there is another group of boys called the Crush 'Em Boys and that your group is beefing with them." They nodded again.

"They started it!" Moochie squealed.

"They started spray painting their names on walls in our neighborhood!" Randy added.

"Then one of them threatened James's cousin!" Troy said.

"So, Rock, I mean James, had to beat him up," Moochie told them.

"Then they beat me up!" Troy scowled.

"We can't let them get away with that!" said Randy.

The principal held up her hand for silence. Just then, there was a knock on the door. Officer Jackson opened it and in walked Coach Jennings.

James's heart sank. He knew that Coach Jennings was about to tell them they could kiss their dreams of being on the basketball team good-bye.

"You should have come to the police." Coach Jennings gestured to Officer Jackson. "Instead, you chose the wrong action and you have to pay the consequences. I hope you young men can make better decisions in the future."

James hardly spoke during the meeting. Grandpa also remained silent. When they were finally headed home in the van, Grandpa asked, "Why, James?"

"I'm sorry, Grandpa. I was just trying to show those boys that we aren't afraid of them! They've been tagging our neighborhood, so we decided to tag theirs!"

"So you go around with those boys calling yourselves 'Rock's Boys' to prove you're big and bad and cause trouble?" Grandpa asked. "Then they come here and cause more trouble! The cycle continues and nothing good comes out of it. Someone could end up hurt or worse! To prove what?"

James sunk down in his seat and folded his arms. All the way home, he tried not to cry.

Grandma met them at the front door. She had on her hotel uniform.

"So what did the school say?" she asked Grandpa.

"He's suspended," Grandpa sighed. "And he has to clean up the graffiti. Officer Jackson will be here Saturday morning to pick him up. I don't know what I'm going to do with him."

James started to climb the stairs. He felt miserable. Then things got worse.

Greg cried, "I wish we weren't cousins!"

James couldn't believe what he heard. "What did you say?"

"I said I wish I wasn't your cousin!" Greg said as he approached the steps. "You're always causing problems! I try hard to bring honor to this family, and you're always messing it up!"

"You're no better than I am, Greg! We are more alike than you think!" James jumped down the stairs and confronted Greg.

Greg stood his ground. He was so angry he couldn't help himself. "Even before the mural you were always the one creating trouble!" Greg hissed.

"Why don't you just leave and never come back?"

"No!" Charles screamed.

James swung and Greg ducked. Greg hit James in the nose before James punched him in the eye. The two went down to the floor.

"Stop it!" April grabbed James. Grandpa came rushing in.

"What's going on?" he roared. He rushed to grab James. Blood flowed from James's nose.

Greg looked up at James and said, "I hate you!"

Without a word, James shrugged off Grandpa and marched out the door. He jumped on his bike and started pedaling. He didn't care where he went. He just couldn't go back to the house.

Forget them all! James thought. Tears streamed down his cheeks. He wasn't paying attention to where he was going.

James stopped his bike when he realized he had pedaled all the way to the supermarket. It was closed, but he saw a couple of people biking by a dumpster over on the side.

At first, James thought they were being nasty, until he recognized a low hissing sound. Then, one of them laughed.

They hadn't seen James, so he decided to sneak up on them. He silently pedaled over. When he got closer, he smiled wickedly at his own luck. Mark was standing yards away with his back turned. Now it was time for revenge.

"This will get Rock's attention!" Mark laughed. He was spraying some very bad words about James and his boys.

"Funny how we're the losers and you two are about to get your butts kicked." James had gotten off his bike without a sound and stood behind them.

They jumped at his words and slowly turned. It was almost worth all the trouble to James to see the looks of terror on their faces.

Even though there were two of them and one of James, both boys took off running and jumped on their bikes. James followed. He pedaled hard, trying to keep up with the boys and hurling insults.

"Y'all are scared now!" James taunted. "You two are nothing but cowards!"

Within minutes they were at the base of the hill. James didn't care. He was going to get Mark if it was the last thing he did! Then he saw five more boys on bikes. They rounded a corner and headed for Mark and James. James knew there would be seven against one, and he didn't like those odds!

They got off their bikes and circled James. James clenched his fists, ready for the worst.

A police siren went off, and a patrol car turned in the direction of the fight. The boys dashed to their bikes.

"You're so lucky!" Mark pointed to James. James silently agreed.

The squad car pulled up alongside James. It was Officer Jackson.

"Get in," was all he said.

James's Plan

It seemed like everyone wanted in on punishing James. Grandpa punished him with no basketball practice. James lost a spot on the basketball team before he even tried out. His principal suspended him from school. On top of that, he had to spend weekends cleaning up graffiti!

"Ugh." James was in bed feeling depressed. He wished there was a way to turn back time and make things right again.

Grandpa knocked on his door, but he didn't come in his room. James groaned as he got ready for the unveiling of Greg's mural when he heard a tap on his window.

James ran over and looked outside. Troy was standing in the front yard. He had a look on his face that meant trouble. James threw the window open.

"What's up?" James asked, scared that Grandpa might hear.

"They beat up Moochie!" Troy looked pale. "We were biking over to Greg's ceremony when four of them followed us. Two of them pushed Moochie off his bike. They kicked him a couple of times before some man yelled that he called the police.

"Moochie's nose is bloody, but he managed to bike over to his brother's house. He said he needed to talk to you."

James was too concerned for Moochie to be scared of Grandpa. He quickly dressed, wrote a note to Grandpa, and climbed out the window to join Troy.

By the time they got to Ken's house, Moochie's clothes looked ruffled, but his nose had stopped bleeding.

"James!" Moochie cried. "Mark pushed me off my bike. He told me he tagged a new message for you. He said that he hopes you like it."

"What message?" James was puzzled.

"He didn't say. But that's not the worst of it!" Moochie looked miserable. "It's where he left the message!"

"Where could he have sprayed it?" James asked, half-jokingly. "My school? On my Grandpa's front door or Greg's mu—" James was out the door in seconds.

No! Not Greg's mural! James felt sick to his stomach, but he kept running. He hoped he wasn't too late.

Greg was already on stage about to pull the rope that would let down the sheet covering his mural. James pushed through the crowd.

"Greg! Wait! Don't pull the rope!" James squeezed through.

Greg noticed James was trying to get his attention. He stopped what he was doing, but the mayor told him to continue. Greg pulled the rope and the sheet fell.

The crowd gasped and fell silent in surprise. The mayor was dumbstruck. Greg looked like he might faint. Mark had sprayed some very bad words about James and Greg on the mural.

James fought the feelings of revenge all the way home. He knew that more tagging and more violence between Mark and his friends would lead to more trouble. He had to try something different. It was time to be a leader.

There has to be a way to make things right, James thought. Then, an idea came to him. But he had to wait.

Greg broke down and cried as soon as they got home. James put an arm around Greg. Greg cried on his shoulder.

"I'm sorry," James's voice cracked. "I found out too late. I didn't want you to see—" he sniffed. "I didn't mean for this to happen."

Greg looked at him. He seemed to know that James meant what he said.

Just then there was a tap on the door. Officer Jackson came in, looked at both

Greg and James, and asked, "Do either of you know anything that can help us find out who did this?"

"It was Mark!" Greg sneered. "I hope you find him before I do!"

"Greg!" Grandpa snapped. "Don't tell me you're thinking about going to find those boys?"

"Why not?" Greg demanded. "It's what James is going to do!" He turned to James. "Right?"

James straightened up and smiled. "Actually, I think we could use a little police help on this one."

Greg's jaw dropped. So did everyone else's in the room. James laughed at everyone's expressions. "I've got a plan!"

Cousins United

The next night, James was preparing to put his idea to work. He dressed in a hurry, ignoring his fear of the dangerous job ahead.

I'm actually glad Grandpa agreed to this! James smiled to himself.

Grandpa entered his room and cleared his throat.

"So," Grandpa sat on his bed, "preparing for your adventure?"

"Yes!" James joked. "I get to put my bad boy skills to work."

Grandpa chuckled despite himself. He patted James's bed. James joined him.

"You probably won't believe me," Grandpa began, "but I was quite the troublemaker in my day."

James's jaw dropped. Grandpa sighed. "Yep. I got into more trouble as an adult. Things were definitely different back when I was younger. There comes a time when a boy has to become a man and fight for things worth fighting for, like getting rid all of the bad in the world. Do you understand?"

James nodded. Grandpa continued. "Greg is fighting in his own way." He put an arm around James. "You are working to change the world for the better, too."

"How?" James asked in disbelief. "Even if I try to do good, something bad always happens, making me end up doing something wrong anyway!"

Grandpa said gently, "You have to keep trying. You managed to persuade your friends to practice ball for weeks without any trouble. It takes a real leader to do that. You just have to decide which direction you're going to go and do your best to stay focused on that direction."

James nodded. He knew Grandpa was right. He just needed to stay focused on doing the right thing and life would work itself out.

Grandpa hugged James. "I am proud of you," Grandpa said. "I will do my best to tell you that more often."

An hour later, James, Greg, and their friends had made their way up the hill. It was now or never. James took a deep breath and walked up to Mark and his friends.

"Mark!" James called. He was glad Mark couldn't see him sweating in the rain. "It's over, Mark. No more tagging in each other's property."

"Oh really?" Mark raised his eyebrows.

James pointed to a video camera under the awning that the boys hadn't noticed. "The police are on their way."

Mark's friends made a move for their bikes. Mark stopped them.

"You're lying!" Mark laughed. "Why would the cops team up with a lowlife like you?"

"Because I no longer want to be a lowlife!" James said. "Tagging our neighborhoods is wrong! Beating each other up is wrong. Don't you want to be a person that people respects?"

"I am getting respect!" Mark bellowed. Mark and his friends moved in closer on James. James rushed for his bike. Moochie, Troy, and Randy were already on their bikes.

"Get out of here!" James told his friends amid the commotion.

"James!" Troy suddenly reappeared. "Moochie said that Greg went down the alley to look for you!"

"No!" James nearly lost his balance on his bike. He jumped off and ran.

It was almost impossible to see through the rain. James was near the group of boys before he knew they were there. He made out silhouettes of four boys surrounding Greg.

"Hey! Leave him alone! Now!" James

yelled.

The boy holding Greg immediately dropped him and ran down the alley. Just then a police car pulled up.

"Are you okay?" James grabbed Greg and looked him in the eyes.

"Yeah, I'm fine." Greg rubbed his back.

Moochie, Troy, and the others were at the police car watching the police arrest the Crush 'Em Boys.

"Yeah! We got y'all!" Moochie bragged. "Now you have to do graffiti cleanup!"

"See you there!" Mark retorted while being placed in a car.

Officer Jackson came over to the boys. He was followed by a woman. "Boys, this is Lieutenant Tracy. She and her

team have been trying to catch those boys for some time."

James laughed. "It was fun hunting down the bad guys! Almost makes me want to be a cop."

They all stopped to stare at him. Officer Jackson's jaw dropped.

"What?" James winked. "A guy can't have a change of heart?"

Making Choices
Greg the Good

Every decision a person makes has a consequence. Greg made some decisions that earned him the nickname Greg the Good. Let's take a look:

Decision: Greg chose to enter a contest to better his community.

Consequence: Greg won and was rewarded with a scholarship and his work on display.

Decision: Greg chose not to get revenge on Mark by tagging neighborhoods.

Consequence: Greg was part of the group that helped catch the taggers!

Making Choices
James the Rock

Every decision has a consequence. James made some decisions that got him in trouble. Let's take a look:

Decision: James chose to get back at the Crush 'Em Boys by tagging their neighborhood.

Consequence: Officer Jackson caught James. James was suspended from school and forced to help clean up the graffiti.

Decision: James decided to work with police to solve a problem instead of taking matters into his own hands.

Consequence: The neighborhood bullies were caught and punished. And James found a new way to handle problems!

About the Author

Thalia Wiggins is a first-time author of children's books. She lives in Washington DC and enjoys imagining all of the choices Greg and James can make.

About the Illustrator

Don Tate is an award-winning illustrator and author of more than 40 books for children, including *Black All Around!*; *She Loved Baseball: The Effa Manley Story*; *It Jes' Happened: When Bill Traylor Started to Draw*; and *Duke Ellington's Nutcracker Suite*. Don lives in the Live Music Capitol of the World, Austin, Texas, with his wife and son.